Little Zeb's

Big Question

Caroline Castle & Sam Childs

Hutchinson

London Sydney Auckland Johannesburg

'How do you go?' said Little Zeb.

'I go

hippety-

"hoppety!"

said the
little green frog.

'How do you go?' asked Little Zeb.

'Me? I go

flippety-

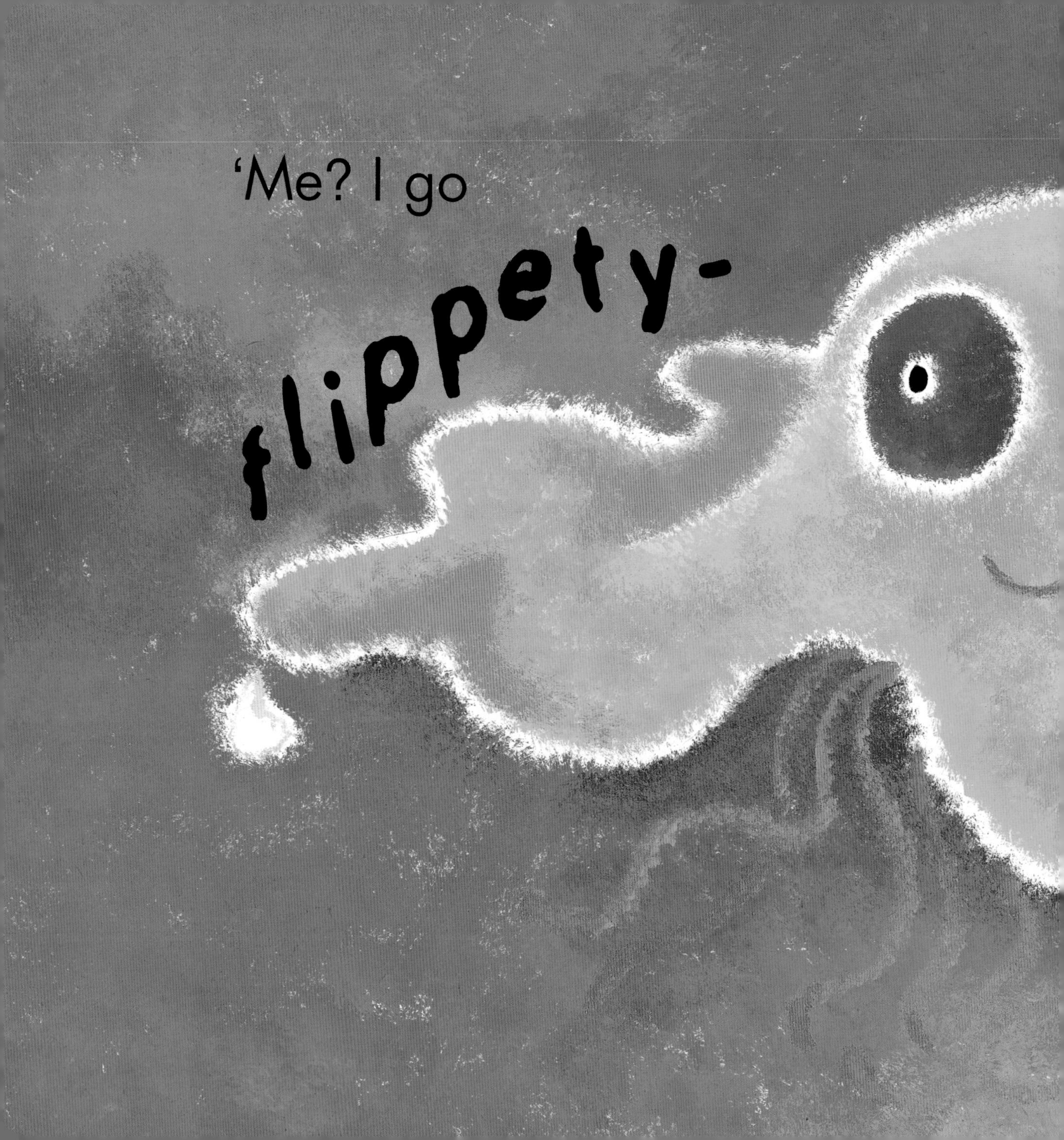

'floppety,'

said the jellyfish.

'How do you go?'
asked Little Zeb.

'Well, I go

bibbity-

bobbity,

said the little brown hare.

'How do you go?' asked Little Zeb.

'Watch me,' said the ostrich.
'I go

lippety

loppity.

'And how do you go?'
asked Little Zeb.

'I go

snippety-snoppety,

snippety...

snap!'

said the
big green crocodile.

'Oh,' said Little Zeb.
'That's when I go

clippety-cloppety, clippety-cloppety